DUM SPIRO, SPERO

A Collection of Stories

GRACE FINNICK MANDERS

*To everyone who has felt hopeless, especially lately
We will persevere* 🤍

CONTENT WARNINGS

There are stories in this collection that cover dark topics. I have done my best to include any relevant content warnings here, but this list may not be conclusive. Stories include discussion of death, sexual assault, and suicidal ideation.

CONTENTS

INTRODUCTION

In 2020, I began work on a collection of short stories that I would go on to publish under the title *growing pains*. At the time, I felt like I had climbed Mount Everest when I pressed the "go live" button for the manuscript. As time went on, I really struggled to appreciate the work that I put into that collection. Like most (maybe all) writers, I go back to read my old work now and find myself overly critical.

I have spent the past 5 years doing my very best to avoid any chatter around that collection, which is a shame, because I should be proud of the work I did on those stories. During these 5 years, however, I have also taken time to work on several different short works when time allows.

Towards the end of 2024, I started to get that itch again to publish some of my work. I sat down to read through all the work I had produced from ages 25 – 29 and tried my damnedest to find a connection point. I needed a title for this collection, and my strategy with *growing pains* was to identify a common theme with all the included works. I finally landed on four main themes – all in some way rooted in hope – to break the collection into, and thus, *Dum Spiro, Spero* was born!

Dum Spiro, Spero is a Latin phrase meaning "while I breath, I hope." I found the title fitting for a lot of reasons. Many of the stories in this collection represent or discuss hope in a literal way, but there are also stories in this collection that carry a more discreet undercurrent of hopefulness. As with *growing pains*, I will warn you that some of the stories in this collection are, uh, depressing. I'm sorry, "write what you know" and all.

This collection is broken down into four main sections: Life, Death, and Everything in Between; Religion and Myth; Love in all its Forms; and Musings on the World. The works included range from lyrical prose to poems to essay-style ramblings. Folks who read *growing pains* will recognize a couple of the titles here as well. (I have unpublished *growing pains* in its original format, but a few of the stories were poignant enough to make the cut for this collection.)

The original title for this collection was "Your Late 20's are Really Fucking Weird." All these works come from places of reflection throughout my late 20s, a time in your life that I am convinced is some sort of liminal space designed to make you question everything that has ever happened in the history of the world. But ultimately, I realized the goal of this collection was to write stories that made me feel strongly about life and the future.

Each section will come with its own introduction to explain why I was thinking about these particular concepts, so I'll keep this section brief.

For anyone who also read *growing pains*, I will end with the same general message: thank you endlessly for choosing my words to read. I am honored to be someone you trust to take you on this journey.

LIFE, DEATH, AND EVERYTHING IN BETWEEN

Everyone contemplates the meaning of life at some point in their lives. I have always been a rather introspective person by nature, so I have spent nearly all my 29 years earth-side thinking about life and what it means to live.

This section really comes from a place of deep grief. Most of the stories in this section were written in the months immediately following the sudden loss of my aunt. I spent many days filled with anger over her sudden departure and, through that, spent many days evaluating my life and everything I'd lived through up to that point.

I promise you that this section is more than doom and gloom. There are also stories here that come from a place of utter wonder of the world around us. They come from places of happiness, contemplation, and gratitude.

Over the past 5 years, I have thought a lot about my life and how I have lived up to this point. There are stories contained in this section that highlight that reflection. Our lives are built on the large moments – weddings, funerals, graduations – but also the small moments – picking flowers in the yard, listening to a new song for the first time. This section is meant to highlight all the moments, big and small, from birth till death.

GRIEF IS STRANGE

it's good to see you
I am drowning in this sorrow

thank you for coming
why does no one else seem angry like me?

your dress looks nice
I barely got to know them

I'll see you at the next one...
why must there always be a next one?

DON'T PANIC, YOU'LL
BE OKAY

The first time it happens, I am sitting in my childhood bedroom, alone and young of age, barely 12 years old. My chest clinches with some unknown anticipation, my brain whirls around me, my thoughts fall away like flour through a sieve.

At the time, I have no words for this sensation, this unending idea that everything is wrong, that I am wrong. Over the next few years, these "attacks" come at what appear to be random moments – the night of my first high school dance, the night I first feel a friendship ending, the night before an exam. I cannot make sense of these moments or why I am burdened with their pain.

Years pass with these attacks fading in and out of my life. Slowly, my childhood fades away, giving into the complexities of adolescence.

It's July. The summer air would feel hot and sticky on my skin if I could bring myself to leave the safety of this same childhood bedroom. I am 17 years old and heartbreak, true heartbreak, has finally found me. Friendships wither around me, lost to the tidal wave of this chest-aching despair. I find myself alone — feeling entirely unlovable — and reeling from both a loss of proximity and a loss of existence.

The walls continue to close in with every passing day. My heart, now a permanently flexed muscle, aches constantly. It has been over a week since I felt the levity of a deep breath. Am I dying?

It is nearly October. My chest is still tight, I am still a mere 17 years old, I am still cut open by my losses, I am staring down the barrel of a loaded gun. The trigger never appealed to me before, but I hear its siren song 24 hours a day — even in my resting moments. I am lost, abandoned to the sea of my negative thoughts. The inevitable pain of the bullets stays my hand.

A less painful way to go, I think, that is what I must find. I am nearly 18 now, have lived in this brutal hell of my mind for 6 relentless years. Every morning, I ask myself how much longer I can survive this life, how much longer I can live with this unnamed illness, this unnamed pain in my heart, my soul.

I am staring at the heap of white circles in my palm when I find them — a stranger, worlds away, a person who also understands this reality, a person who lives in this hell along-side me.

Panic attacks, anxiety, they tell me. My condition, my painful friend I have nearly learned to live with, has a name. This constant ache inside me has a cure. I am no longer alone in this battle. My enemy has a name, a consistent form I can anticipate. I know my enemy's tactics, and I ready my defenses against them.

I am 18 years old, staring at the pile of white circles in my hand. I am 18 years old, learning that I am not alone in this fight. I am 18 years old, slowly pouring those circles back into their orange container, fastening the lid, placing them back in the medicine cabinet.

I am 35 years old, still battling that old foe. I am 35 years old, never once thinking of reaching for that pill bottle. I am

35 years old and eternally grateful for the 18-year-old version of myself that reached out for help. I am 35 years old, still fighting off these chest clenching pains, but able to look out into the wide horizon that holds my future. I am 35 years old and, for the first time, see myself growing gray hairs.

DRIVING WITH THE
WINDOWS DOWN

When I was a little girl, my dad would take me for rides in his truck. Sometimes these rides were purposeful - we needed to take the trash to the compactor or run to the grocery store. But sometimes we would just go just for the sake of riding around and enjoying the weather. My favorite rides were always the ones in early October. The weather would be chilly but not yet cold. We'd crank the manual windows down, wrap up in light jackets, and let the falling leaves fly in the window. Occasionally, a leaf would fly through the window to attack, and we'd share a laugh.

Our favorite ride soundtrack was the local classic rock station. Sometimes we'd mix things up and listen to one of our favorite cassettes - Lynyrd Skynyrd's debut album or Dark Side of the Moon by Pink Floyd. Growing up, these rides just seemed like a good way to spend time with my father outside of our home. I never imagined that riding around in a car would become a cherished memory.

I was a fresh college grad and working from home at the time. Every weekday during lunch I'd run to the gym to get in a quick workout. Work always waited impatiently for me to return from my lunch break, so I usually took the quickest route possible: down the interstate, flooring it the entire way. My windows stayed rolled up and the radio usually ran through whatever random playlist I had clicked that day. There was no real enjoyment in my rides to and from the gym. I saw them as a mission that needed to be completed as quickly as possible.

Even outside of my gym trips, I never took the time to slow down. Trips to the grocery store or friends' homes were always via the fastest route possible. The windows stayed shut and I kept my self locked into the air-conditioned cab. I spent every drive holed up in the car, never rolling down the windows.

One sunny October Saturday, I woke expecting to spend my day running errands – grocery shopping and such. As I walked to my car, I felt the cool breeze rustle through my hair and watched the leaves slowly fall from their branches. The weather had dropped from a muggy 85 to a crisp 65 degrees overnight in true Georgia fashion.

I walked back inside, wrapped in a light jacket, and readied myself for a moment of nostalgia. As I backed out of my parking space, thoughts of those drives with my dad ran through my brain. Without even thinking about it, I turned left towards the backroads route instead of going straight onto the highway that day. While stopped at a red light, I turned on more purposeful music – Dark Side of the Moon – and rolled the windows down.

This wasn't the same as the memories of my childhood. The music sang perfectly from the speakers and played from a Bluetooth connection instead of crackling through a tape – my car didn't even have a cassette player. And my windows rolled down with the push of a button instead of having to crank them down myself. Yet, some sense of calm washed over me in a tsunami-like wave.

My plans to quickly knock out my errands was derailed by my stroll down memory lane. I wove through the streets of my unfamiliar town - suddenly realizing I hardly knew my way around the place I'd lived in for nearly a year now. My car took me south until I felt I should turn back, but I didn't go back home, I kept driving north towards more unfamiliar roads. I suddenly needed to just ride around and enjoy the weather.

As I drove, leaves started flying through my open windows, creating a pile on the passenger side floorboards and seat. At one point I got hit in the face by one particularly eager leaf and laughed - some aspects of my drives with my father would never truly change. As I continued following the curves of the road, I found a good stopping place - a parking lot designated for people that ran the river trail. I wouldn't be running, but the leaves fell in earnest here and all I needed was to watch them shower down.

The Chattahoochee rushed down its path, and I let my brain get lost in its ebbs and flows – following the leaves on their journey downstream. I reminisced on the many changes that had occurred since my childhood – the natural distance that had grown between my father and I, the adult responsibilities that now piled up in my life, the job I now worked each day. My life had changed immensely in the ten plus years since my last ride with my father. Sometimes there was nothing I desired more than to go back in time and yell at my younger self to appreciate the little things more and stop worrying about the future. But here I sat as a mostly functioning adult, so I didn't complain.

The wind picked up, and a shiver rolled through my spine – time to go back home. I returned to my car, rolled down my windows, and picked a playlist before putting the car in reverse. It may have been more than a decade since the last time I rode casually in the truck with my father, but nothing would ever take away the feeling I got when I drove with my windows down.

MADE OF MOMENTS

Every person you know is a walking collection of memories. We pass one another on the street, having no idea the struggles or joys rattling around each other's minds.

The girl you sit next to on the subway just ended her decade long relationship. The woman that calls you "baby" at the supermarket checkout struggles daily with the loss of her son. The man in front of you in line at the coffee shop orders the chocolate chip frozen drink for his daughter as a reward for her report card grades. The person you stand next to on the street corner, the one with the extra-bright smile, just learned that insurance will cover their gender-affirming surgery.

Everyone around us carries a story. Maybe the story currently running in their mind brings them joy or maybe it makes it harder for them to be out and about. We never truly know what is going on in the lives of those around us, not even those we call our closest friends.

The friend that cancelled lunch for the third time in a month lost a pregnancy. It was too early to tell you in the first place, so it's that much harder for her to explain herself now. Instead, she buries herself in the guilt of constantly cancelling and the feelings of sadness and failure that come from a soundless exam room.

Your sister seems happier than normal because she just planned the perfect surprise weekend for the two of you. She's doing her best to seem casual, and you know that something has her smiling so big. But she'll brush it off as just having a good day. She obviously can't come right out and admit the real root of her happiness.

Everyone, from the people you pass innocuously in the dairy aisle to the friends and family you see on a regular basis, tries their best every day to handle the cards in their current hand. And at the end of it all, we tally up the wins and losses and (hopefully) all rejoice at the lives we share.

I am made of moments – moments of triumph, moments of loss, moments of love, moments of great joy, moments of sadness, moments of anger, moments enjoyed alone, moments shared with friends.

I like to think that, somewhere, exists a scrapbook of my life. It tallies the moments and creates great mosaics of my best days – a highlight reel of my favorite times. At the end of it all, I hope my scrapbook strains its bindings, I hope it grows so full of joy and love that I'm forced to expand into a second volume.

Like everyone around me, I am made of moments, and these moments are made of me.

RELIGION AND MYTH

I fear that overthinking your beliefs is an inevitable rite of passage in your life. And with that overthinking, I personally believe in reading as much as possible to both affirm and deny the things you choose to believe in.

Questioning my religion is a practice I hope to keep for the rest of my life. I personally believe that it's *healthy* to do so and to invite other belief systems into your bucket of information.

Over the past 5 or so years, I have read countless tales of religious allegory and general myth. Through those readings, there were a few stories that stuck with me and made me think about my own perspectives. There are also stories that made me wonder how true the retellings were.

This section is dedicated to the stories I read that make me think critically about myself and my place in the world. None of these stories are truly factual, and I do not ever claim to be a historical expert in any of these topics. If you're someone who would be angered by someone re-interpreting stories from the Bible in a more feminist and/or modern fashion (or by someone simply taking creative liberties with certain tales), I advise you to skip "In the Garden" and "One Mortal Moment." If you are someone who would be angered by the reinterpretation of Greek myth and reframing certain characters in a new (and at times divisive) light, I advise you to skip "Still, I Fly" and "I Choose the Snakes."

In a way, these stories are the odd balls of the collection. They're less a commentary on hope or humanity in a direct or tangible way, and they're instead about the different stories we hear as children and how those stories reframe themselves as we grow older. These stories originated the collection. They were the stories I read back and thought "there's something here worth saying."

While these stories may not address the concept of hope in a direct way, my reinterpretations of the Greek myths are designed to take tales that initially seem bleak and turn them into hopeful endings. On the other side, my reinterpretation of the biblical stories takes tales that have historically been regarded in one light while I offer up an opposing viewpoint, ultimately humanizing the characters of the bible in many ways.

When I decided to include these stories, I hoped they would accomplish two main things: to make others think critically about their world views and the stories they've accepted as fact throughout the years, and to serve as more realistic (and at times, optimistic) versions of traditionally frustrating or sad stories. While I know these won't be for everyone, I hope you enjoy them.

IN THE GARDEN

My eyes open to see a wide, beautiful garden. There is another one like me lingering nearby. *Adam*, my God tells me. *This is Adam, and he has helped me create you. You are Eve.*

Eve. This must be my name. I do not quite understand yet where I am, but I feel at peace. Lush vegetation sprawls in every direction. Animal calls create a symphony in this idyllic space.

I am not aware of much; I do not yet know how to feel about anything. My God tells me that I am happy, that I am cared for, that I am to build out humanity on this great Earth. He warns Adam and I both to not eat the pomegranate, to not indulge in the tree of knowledge. He promises to care for us and to be our guide. I know that if anything in this garden were to happen, He would be the one to orchestrate it. My God is all knowing, all caring, and all just.

Adam and I appear to be equals in many ways. We stand eye to eye with one another, both bearing the same light brown skin. He is harder in areas that I am softer. His body does not bear the fleshier parts I seem burdened to carry around. Neither of us understands yet our role in this world.

He tells me that God took one of his bones to create me – I am expected to be nothing but grateful for this gift.

Days pass us by. Adam and I lay together each night and wander during the days. We do not question anything around us – our God ensures we have no need of knowledge, that we must continue to enjoy Eden, never straying to that pomegranate tree.

I am in the garden when I first hear his voice. *Come closer, my child, let me see you.* I know that my God watches me, that he guides me through this new and strange world. I know my God is all knowing, kind, and always looking to keep me safe. The voice is not my God's. He has not spoken to me since the moments after my creation.

The voice lures me further into the garden – *my precious child, I have much I need you to see.* I turn the corner to see a large serpent standing next to a tree. Not just a tree, I realize, the pomegranate tree, the tree that would teach me the ways of this world. My God previously told me to never approach this tree, but the serpent is also of His creation. If everything in this garden comes from my Creator and His will, then I should trust everything within Eden.

This is my first encounter with the serpent. I stay closer to our den each day, while Adam roams further. Out of all of God's creations, this serpent remains the most unique. He – or I believe it to be a male, his voice carries the same deep timber of Adam's - stands on 4 legs, a large tail slithers behind him, and a male-like head rests atop a long neck.

You are beautiful, the serpent tells me. It moves languidly around the tree, stepping carefully as to not burst any of the fallen fruit.

"Who are you? I do not believe we have crossed paths before now," I ask.

My name is of no importance, sweet child. I have come here to see you, to give you a message from our dear Creator. To let you know of changes he wishes to make to Eden. The serpent smiles at me.

Something in the back of my mind warns to be wary, but God would not create this creature to intentionally deceive me, my God loves me. After all, when He created me, He promised to always watch over and protect me. He would not allow an imposter to enter Eden. He would not allow for someone to forsake me and lead me astray.

The serpent edges closer, passing behind me and wrapping his long neck along my midsection, stretching up to gaze into my eyes. *My dearest Eve, the time has finally come for you to eat of the pomegranate tree. God would like you, Eve, to teach Adam of this world. Be the light in this world and teach others of true good and evil.*

"But Father said I would perish should I eat from this tree," I cry. "He said it would bring about my death."

My sweet child, do not fret. He merely said this to frighten you. You will not come to harm from eating the pomegranate seeds. You will simply gain a new understanding of Eden. This will make you more like God. The serpent smiles at me.

I give a moment's hesitation before untwining myself from the serpent. Stretching onto my toes, I reach for the succulent, deep-red fruit. The pomegranate almost seems to pulse in my hand, aware that this small creation is about to change the trajectory of my life, change the trajectory for all mankind. My arm acts of its own accord, peeling back the soft skin, allowing the membrane to fall away and the bright, juicy seeds to present themselves to me. Guided by my Father's wisdom, I bring this fruit to my mouth, breaking off but a few seeds in the process.

Adam enters the clearing as I swallow. The serpent explains to him that all is okay, that God has asked this of us, to eat of the fruit tree. I peel back more of the soft membrane of the fruit, noticing just how red the juice is – it reminds me of blood. I bring the pomegranate to Adam's mouth, allowing him a bite no larger than my own.

The serpent fades away in a cloud of smoke. Suddenly, I

am gripped with self-consciousness. Naked, I am naked. And Adam is naked. And we should not be standing here, in the open, naked. This is quite improper.

Adam joins in my blushing, and we quickly fasten leaves into makeshift coverings. One each for our lower bodies and two for my chest.

Suddenly, the garden begins to rumble. The sky blackens. God approaches, wrath and anger marring His once peaceful face.

"EVE". My father shouts. "How dare you break my one rule? How dare you forsake me? And you would drag Adam into your misdeeds as well; you would tarnish his soul alongside yours?"

"Please, Father," I beg. "I have been tricked. The serpent, he insisted you wanted me to eat the fruit. He promised this was important. He claimed you wished for me to learn of this world!"

"You foolish child. You disgrace me, Eve," he says. Disgrace him? How was I to know the serpent was an enemy? How is my name the only one on his tongue in admonishment when Adam stands next to me, guilty of the same sins.

Deceived. Thoroughly and utterly deceived. My Father, my protector, my God. He abandoned me to this folly. He watched, he saw, he let me be fooled. He says he is all knowing, but if he is all knowing then why would he allow me to fall into this trap? Why would he allow the serpent to carry such lies?

I sit by as this god doles out his punishments, as he shames me for falling into this trap. He insists he has delivered equal punishment among the three of us. But this god, this creature I used to believe loved me, he levies his punishments quickly and mercilessly. He has decided that I am the larger one to blame. He will hear nothing of my abandonment, he will not hear of the serpent's trickery, he will not entertain that Adam would have easily been fooled as well, he will not accept even an ounce of blame. My all-knowing, all-protecting god gone, replaced with this menacing and spiteful being.

He punishes Adam by cursing the land. Adam's punishment becomes mine as well since I must also eat the fruits of his labor. He strips the serpent of his legs and human-like features, still allowing this creature to roam the gardens, only taking from him the power of speech. When he turns to me and levies my punishment, I am left in shock. *Unbearable pain to birth children, an act you are expected to participate in. Adam, your husband, shall rule over you. All women shall be ruled by their husbands.*

The serpent slithers away, and God casts me and Adam out of Eden. I become a cautionary tale, relegated to being nothing more than a breeder and a lesson in the story. As I stare at the stars in my final days, I hope that my descendants break my curse, that I have not – unintentionally – become some symbol of wrongness. That I have not truly doomed all women to this life of servitude and suffering. That I have not doomed generations of women through my actions.

ONE MORTAL MOMENT

The bread breaks easily in my hands. I pass pieces along to each of my twelve brothers before me. Wine flows from the carafe into their waiting cups. Passover nears its end, and, with it, I know my time on Earth is coming to a close.

Despite having the knowledge of what is to come, I find myself, for a moment, feeling bitter anger. As I gaze around the room, my eyes continue to drift to the man that will be my downfall. Even here, in this sacred moment, his pockets lie heavier with the coins inside them, his earnings for deceiving me.

I have known, of course, what my ending would be all along. Despite that, I allow myself this mortal moment, this moment of feeling frustration and anger for what I am called to do. Sure, my death brings about salvation for the rest of humankind, but am I truly expected to feel not even a moment of sadness or anger for this great sacrifice?

We sit around this table, and I offer up pieces of myself to each of my brethren. I teach them of the gift I am bestowing, explain to them how to give this gift to others who see the truth through me. I watch as they each take in these gifts, even the one who betrays me. Judas swallows with the rest of them, earning his salvation.

In some ways, we have Judas to thank for this moment, this eternal resting place opening to all men on earth. Judas Iscariot – disciple, friend, brother, son. He who betrays me really gets the credit for my sacrifice. I wonder how my final days would have been had Judas not sold my life to the priests.

In two days' time, I will find myself staked to a cross, dying a painful death so that men may rest peacefully in Heaven. Judas thinks himself righteous, he thinks what he is doing is the right path forward. I cannot blame him. All men have their weaknesses.

As the night draws to a close, I relay the news of what is to come to those at this last dinner. They refuse to accept the truth I have spoken. They cannot fathom that I have been deceived, that I truly mean every word spoken tonight. I have given them the gift of my salvation, shown them how to share in my body and blood. Soon, I will stare down my death. Soon, I will be sealed away in a tomb and waiting to rise again.

These men who I have come to love as brothers share in a final holiday with me. We enjoy each other's company and share in stories of our lives and progress being made in my name, in my Father's name.

My feelings oscillate between anger, sadness, and contentedness. My friend sold me away for a pocket full of silver, I am to be crucified and given a horrific death, I have done what my Father guided me to do and have saved the good people of Earth. In the end, I school my feelings into those of happiness – if I am to die to save all of humanity, then there shall be honor in that death.

The night's ending draws ever nearer. I reflect on the years I spent among these men. History will remember me as a savior while Judas will become synonymous with treason and treachery. As I walk towards my Father and away from man, I hope that my name and my mission on earth remains a story of kindness and hope. I hope that generations from now, my brothers and sisters remember to love each other, regardless of who they are or what they believe.

Together, with my friends, I share in a final toast to this life. With all my knowledge shared, I walk away knowing I go to serve a greater purpose. I go to prepare a place for all.

STILL, I FLY

It begins with the wails of Queen Pasiphae. "My son, my boy," she yells. I hear her from my chambers, calling out for Asterion.

"I wonder what's happened," I ask my father. Turning to face him, his face is an equal mask of sorrow and fear. "What have you done?"

"That will be the Queen crying out for the Minotaur, I imagine. Ariadne gave Theseus my advice after all." My father, Crete's great inventor, looks at me with resignation. "The king will know that I caused this. I am the only one, after all, who knew the tricks of my labyrinth."

Shouts echo down the hall. I hear King Minos, his voice growing closer and closer. The door flies open, and I stand face-to-face with what must be the entire guard of the island of Crete.

"Arrest them both," the king states. Guards rush into the room, securing my father and I both.

"Not my son. Please, sir. My son is innocent in all of this, leave him be," my father pleads. A guard punches him in the mouth and warns him to keep quiet.

We're led through the entire building. Minos plans to

make a statement with our arrest. My friends, Ariadne most of all, watch on with a mix of shame, horror, and pity on their faces. Eventually, we find ourselves in a tower, a makeshift prison for my father and I, where we will await punishment for our crimes.

I feel the loss of my agency almost instantly. My life on Crete has always been one of imprisonment, but in the manor, I could walk the halls, journey to the beach, or chat with other members of the household. Here in this tower, the only view to the outdoors is through a singular window. Two beds and a workstation line the walls. The lone window is, at least, large and opens to allow air into the space.

Our days pass in relatively silence. My father works on new inventions for the king, hoping to buy our freedom, I assume. As the days turn into weeks turn into months, my father grows restless. He mutters to himself most days while huddling over his desk, working on some new design. I keep myself busy by studying his finished drawings and working to understand his mind a little better.

Several months pass like this, with nothing of note happening for either of us. Until one morning, I awake to see my father pacing around our chamber, muttering nonsense to himself about his latest design.

"Freedom, my son. I will get us freedom. Soon, I promise. My work is nearly complete. Then we leave for a new start," he claims. I think him entirely mad. Our time in this cursed tower has ruined his mind. The days pass slowly. I spend my time thinking of the palace we once enjoyed. Thinking of everything I saw in my time there. From the beautiful princess Ariadne to the sunsets on the beach.

One dreary morning, my father finally calls to me, "Son, come help me with this, I'm nearly finished." I rise and walk over to his workspace and stop dead in my tracks when I see his latest creation. Wings. Giant, human-sized wings, looking like they'd been stripped from a game bird and enlarged.

"What on Earth do you expect to do with these?" I couldn't hide the bewilderment from my voice. My father's mind had finally given up; he was officially insane.

"This is the answer, Icarus. This is how we get our freedom." He explains his plan in grand detail to me. "You wear the wings using this harness." He demonstrates how to strap my arms and chest securely into the contraption. "We'll leave through the window just past first light."

Excitement hesitantly builds in my chest. *Maybe this will work. My freedom flies at dawn.* I choose to believe in my father's mad dream. As night approaches, I grow increasingly restless, aching to feel the breeze on my face once more.

Sleep must finally claim me at some point. My father wakes me as the sun crests the horizon. He gives me a final walk through of our plan.

"We'll fly south, over the sea. Follow my lead, son, and we'll be safe and free men by nightfall." He places a hand on my shoulder. "Remember son, you cannot fly too close to the water, or you risk the feathers getting wet and weighing you down. And you cannot fly too high, or the sun will melt the wax away."

With my father's warnings fresh in my mind, we wait for our moment to arrive. My mind races with possibility. A free man, for really the first time in my life. I can walk the markets and buy treats for myself. I can explore dens and taverns, seeking a life partner to share my days with. Music, art, books, even work all light the path of my future.

My father rises, perching himself in the windowsill, and checks his harness once more.

"I will see you on the other side, my son," he says before diving from the window. I climb up after him, taking a moment to watch him soar away.

I check my harness, each of the six arm straps and the chest fastening. I take a moment to memorize this tower, this cell, this prison, and then I move my gaze out to the endless blue sea. Just over the sound of the waves, I hear my father calling for me to hurry.

With one last glance back and a deep breath, I jump from the window. The wind rushes up to greet me like a long-separated lover. A smile breaks across my face, so wide it makes my cheeks ache. Tilting the wings, I rush forward to meet up with my father.

"Remember Icarus, maintain your height and follow me closely. We'll land in the new world soon," he calls to me. I shine him another smile, and he meets me with one of his own.

I'm flying, soaring, rushing into the wind and away from the prison of my old home. Euphoria fills my body with anticipation, restlessness. Months, I had spent months locked in that tower. Freedom smells like salt-water, feels like warm sunshine and a cool breeze. *Just a little higher, let's feel more sun, chase more wind,* my mind whispers. Who am I to deny myself the simple pleasures of this life?

Too long, I had to lock away my desires for too long, but now I am free, I can chase these dreams. I tilt my wings up, just slightly and rise closer to the sky. The sun warms my skin. I close my eyes and take in every small sensation. I hear bird song as they soar alongside me. I feel the warm sun on my face and the cool breeze flowing through my hair. I smell the salt water far below me.

I laugh. I laugh and laugh and laugh and tilt my wings ever higher. Distantly, I hear my father's voice. I feel the warmth of the sun growing stronger. I smell the soft scent of melted wax. I hear the water growing louder, feel sharp points of liquid warmth along my back and arms. My body spins and I am caught in a storm of feathers. Their soft fibers caressing me as they stream towards the great endless sky. Falling, I am falling. Plummeting, really.

My father calls my name; it sounds like a plea. And still, I laugh and laugh. At least in these final moments, I get to fly.

I CHOOSE THE SNAKES

This man holds my head, triumphant. He has slain the great monster feared by all mortal men, he emerges triumphant, ready to return to Athens with my Gorgon head. He thinks me no more than a monster, but I know the truth.

Not long ago, I walked the streets of Greece as a free and beautiful woman. Like all women, I carried a healthy fear of the gods, particularly the brothers – Zeus, Poseidon, and Hades. They ruled the sky, sea, and underworld with zeal and were all known to lure women away. Of course, those women always faced the consequences while the men continued their tyrannical ruling.

I kept my distance from all males, but the brothers I avoided at all costs. I dedicated myself to Athena. I found her strength awe-inspiring, I thought that I, too, could wield power over men and stop living in fear of them. In my wildest dreams, I became a confident and sure woman, a woman who walked the streets at any time of day without fear in her heart, a woman who demanded what she wanted instead of hoping for a stroke of luck.

The days passed by, and I felt myself grow in this confidence, felt myself become this feared woman. I gained the respect of my goddess and thanked her endlessly. Athena was my protector.

Or so I thought.

Despite my constant vigilance, the day eventually arrived where I found myself confronted with one of the brothers, Poseidon. I stood in Athena's temple, preparing to make my monthly offerings and leave prayers behind. He entered the temple in complete silence.

One moment, I faced the altar. The next, Poseidon's hands gripped my hips with a bruising force. *I am not a timid creature anymore,* I thought, *I will not fear this man.* I pushed him away, but his grip only tightened. Panic gripped me, my body numbed, my mind emptied. *Athena protect me,* I thought.

He took what he wanted from me. He dirtied my body, my skin. He filled me with a despair that would never go away. He finished himself off and left me there – to die, to suffer, to just get up and go back about my day?

Finally, Athena arrived. *I'll be okay, she will help me.* Athena's face showed nothing but rage. Confused, I pushed myself up to face her. A disgrace, she called me. A *whore*. I begged, pleaded, with her. *He snuck in here and took what he wanted of me. I would never disrespect you in this way, my goddess.* She heard nothing of my pleas.

Athena unleashed her wrath on me. Blinding pain split my skull in two and knocked me unconscious.

I awoke in my home hours or days or weeks later. I made for the door, seeking fresh air to calm my lungs and grass to cool my feet. A small hiss stopped me in my tracks. I turned slowly to the mirror.

A demon stared back at me. Long gone was my beautiful black hair, long gone was my rosy complexion. In its place was a monster with snakes for hair and ghost-like skin. I wrapped a scarf around my head, thinking to confront Athena for this and once again beg for mercy.

As I skulked through the town center, I tried in earnest to

go unnoticed. A man bumped into, though, and when he gazed upon me, he abruptly turned to stone. The statuesque man crashed over, pieces of stone scattered everywhere. Screams tore out from the crowd, and I ran as fast as I could.

I ran and ran and ran. Eventually, I found this cave. It held just enough space for me to make a den, to carve out some small space for myself.

Years passed in this cave. Athena eventually visited me and admitted what she had done. *Gorgon*, she called me. Snakes for hair and eyes that turned all men to stone. She thought to strip me of the pleasure she assumed I sought in Poseidon. Instead, she granted me power I always desired. I asked after Poseidon, I wanted to know what punishment he faced.

Nothing, of course. Men were not punished for their crimes; it was the woman's responsibility.

Time crept along. Men sometimes wandered into my area. I began to relish their appearances. Sure, Poseidon walked free, but others like him paid the price for him.

Until the day that *this* man showed up. Perseus, he called himself. He darted around; a mirror held out in front of him. He knew me, it seemed. He knew my one flaw. Eventually, he made his final move and removed my head clean from my body.

And now we're here, where I began this tale. Perseus, thinking himself important and brilliant, takes my head away from my home. I live alongside him as he takes my head across the world, turning his own enemies to stone, using me as his own personal weapon.

I lie in this satchel and wait. I know the day will come when Perseus is too comfortable around me. He thinks I am just a head, but I am here, waiting on his folly.

It takes decades, but the day finally arrives. Perseus arrives home and leaves my head stashed away. It's not long after that a child wanders into this room. A tiny hand closes around the linen covering me. Later, a woman's scream rings out, and two bodies worth of stone cover the cupboard floor.

Finally, he arrives. Perseus looks at the destruction around him and glances up, forgetting I am here. *Finally*, I think. The bastard turns to stone, and I smile.

LOVE IN ALL ITS FORMS

I am, in fact, a hopeless romantic. I *love* love – platonic love, familial love, romantic love. Any kind of love, give it to me.

This section started when I wrote the story "Girls, Together." My friend has recently gotten engaged and asked me to be a bridesmaid in her wedding. One night, as I reflected on our highly entertaining and strange path to best-friendship, I sat down and tried putting into words how she made me feel. From there, more stories about my loved ones or about love in general started pouring out of me.

This section remains the happiest set of stories I've ever written – with the small exception of "Obsessive Compulsive Love," but if you've read *growing pains* then you already know what to expect with that one.

Love is the best part of being human. It's the thing that gets us through the darkest of days. Love for my family and friends and husband keep me going when the going gets tough.

I wanted to bottle up some of that love and display it

here. I hope as you read these stories, you think of the ones you love in your own life. There is a story here for all three of the categories I listed earlier. So, sit back and enjoy some sappy stories straight from my big mushy heart and call your loved ones to tell them you love them today.

MIDNIGHT LOVER

I still hear your voice
look at the moon.
I run from my bed
and look up at the rock in the sky
but I do not see the moon
I see you
and all your love
and relish how you think of me
when you gaze into the night

OBSESSIVE COMPULSIVE LOVE

She left on a Tuesday. I didn't think I had done anything wrong that day. In fact, I knew that there was nothing that I could have done wrong. I made sure to make the bed – I made it five times. And I knew I turned off the lights – 17 times to be exact, I counted. When I kissed her goodbye that morning, I knew it had to be perfect. I had to redo the kiss six times to make sure that it was exactly right – our lips had to line up perfectly. Perfectly.

She told me it wasn't my fault; she said that she just needed to have her own space for a while. She promised that I never did anything wrong, but somehow that was the problem. I didn't understand. I tried so hard. I loved her so much. So much.

It's always been this way. Even when I was younger. I tried to play football in high school – I was going to be a kicker, but my coach told me to "piss off" because I kept telling him that I couldn't kick the ball if it wasn't placed perfectly on the tee. I told him that I cared. He told me I cared too much and couldn't stay any longer. I cared too much. Too much.

My mom took me to a doctor once and he told me I have "OCD." According to him, lots of people had it and it was totally normal. My entire life revolved around my diagnosis. When I went to summer camps, everyone would treat me funny, like I was going to explode any minute and begin micromanaging their lives. When I got to high school, my teachers commended me for how neat and tidy my work was – everything I turned in was perfect. My teachers always got mad at me because many times, I didn't turn in my assignments when they were due. When they asked me why, I always told them that I hadn't had the time to perfect them yet, but I would turn them in very soon. They never understood; they always told me that whatever I could get done was good enough. They didn't understand. I didn't want "good enough," I needed it to be perfect. Perfect.

When I met her, I instantly knew she was the one. She laughed when I turned the lights on and off 17 times before coming to bed, and her face always brightened with joy with each consecutive kiss – she thought I was great just for wanting to make sure the kiss was done right. As time went on, I started to notice that she didn't laugh when I turned off the lights those 17 times. And she started to get annoyed when I was just trying to kiss her correctly. One day, she left before I could give her a perfect kiss – I waited all day for her to come home so that I could finally fix it. All I wanted in life was to please her, make her feel special. So special.

I bought her a ring. I was still trying to plan the perfect proposal in my head. I was going to propose in September. I wanted to propose somewhere perfect – maybe in a park where we had walked before, or in a restaurant that I knew would get the food right. Once I decided on a place and date – at the Italian restaurant down the road, on September 20th at 9:32pm exactly – I bought a ring. She would have loved this ring; it was perfect. Absolutely perfect.

The night she left, I begged her to stay just one more night, but she said that she needed to get some sleep; she had a big presentation at work that morning. She said that she couldn't wait for me to turn off the lights 17 times; she said that she couldn't wait for me to get a perfect kiss. She told me that she would stay if I only turned off the lights once. She told me she would stay if I just kissed her like a "normal" person and let her go to sleep. But I couldn't do it. How could I let the love of my life go to bed without getting a perfect kiss from me? How?

Ever since she left, I haven't slept through the night. My thoughts keep me awake, wondering what I could have done better. I call her multiple times, every day. Every time I call her, I have something new to say. Usually the first call consists of me wishing her a good day at work, then the next few calls will revolve around how I wish I could be with her, wish I could kiss her again, and most days the last few calls are just me crying on one end, begging her to tell me what I did wrong. I tell her that I love her exactly five times every time I call, no more, no less. No less.

When we began dating, she used to ask me lots of questions. She told me that she never meant to be rude, but she wanted to understand why I was the way I am. I always told her that I didn't really know why I was this way, but she was determined to understand me more; she said that if she could listen to me talk about my brain, then she would begin to understand it. After months of talking and questioning, she promised that she understood. She said that she loved my antics, she said that she loved me. I loved her too. I loved her so much. I still love her.

Some days I was able to act "normal." I could turn the lights off 10 times instead of 17 and still go to sleep. I could accept a great kiss instead of a perfect one. I could make the bed three times instead of five. These days were the best for us. She would commend me for doing so good and remind me that it was okay for me to be myself, even if it meant being slightly annoying to her. She always recognized my progress, but right before she left, she stopped noticing the days that I only turned off the lights 10 times, she just noticed that it was more than once and that it was a nuisance. I'm the nuisance.

When she left, I tried going to therapy. I thought that maybe I would feel better once I talked about what happened to us. But my therapist didn't care about me winning her back, he just told me that I needed to focus on myself. I don't want to focus on myself. I want to focus on her. She was the reason I got up in the morning, the reason I made the bed five times, the reason I turned the lights on and off over and over again until we started to get a headache. She was the reason.

When she left, a piece of me left. I stopped listening to my brain. I lived in a state of madness and chaos. I hated myself and I struggled with the disorder around me. Without her, I saw no reason to even try to be perfect. She was the only one who ever understood me. She was the only one who cared if I thought things were perfect. She understood.

The day she left, I didn't make the bed, not even once. I laid in the unmade bed and screamed and cried and felt the worst pain I had ever felt. The voice in my head was screaming at me to make the bed, telling me that disorder was not okay. Disorder was not okay. It was not okay. But disorder was all I felt. I felt the little people protecting my heart running in circles trying to hold it all together, but I had given up, letting my heart shatter into a million pieces. It could never be fixed. I could never be fixed. I was broken. Broken.

I feel a little better now that a few months have passed. Going to the park doesn't sting like it once did. I made the bed again; five times like I used to. I've become myself again. At first, life without her was the worst thing that I had ever experienced. But somehow this disease made me realize that I am better on my own. It helped me find comfort in my weird urges and desires and needs. My friends don't really come around anymore, but I don't mind. I don't mind.

Before I met her, I hated my brain. I thought that no one would ever love me. Then she entered my life, and I realized that maybe there was someone out there who could love a mess like me. During the time we spent together, I had never felt so alive. She reminded me daily that everyone is a little crazy, some just have a harder time dealing with it. When she walked out that morning, I felt incredible pain. It took me months to look past the pain, but looking back, I'm glad she left. She made me realize that my disease does not entirely define my life. There will be someone else out there who loves me, I'm sure of it. I deserve love.

Today, I decided to go get coffee. I wanted to sit alone in a small shop and maybe talk to a few people around me. I desired new friendships. I wanted to find someone that would love me the way she used to. I think I'm finally healthy again. I think I'm ready to move on. I think.

I got ready this morning and put on my best shirt and jeans – I ironed them three times each just to make sure that they looked perfect. I brushed my hair ten times, making sure that each hair was where it belonged. I had to retie my shoes seven times - can't have the laces uneven. As I walked down the road to the coffee shop, I thought of all the times that she used to take me there. It was her favorite place to visit. I started to think more about her, but I reminded myself not to do that. Every time I thought about her too long, I would call her again, I would stop being me. I would hurt.

I sat at the coffee shop for hours trying to convince myself to say hello to some of the people around me. Finally, I spotted a beautiful woman sitting across the room from me and decided that this was my chance to move on. This was my chance to forget about the pain in my past. The shaking in my hands only got worse the closer I got, but I kept walking. Just kept walking.

I really thought I made the right decision walking up to this woman. I thought that she was the new love of my life, but when I got over to her and she looked up at me with those beautiful blue eyes and those lips that deserved the perfect kiss, I realized who it was. No.

She smiled softly and said hello, but I couldn't move. Here she was. Again. My brain was racing. Telling me to run, to stay, run, stay. Run. Stay. She started to apologize for never returning my calls and that's when I ran. I ran all the way down the street, past my house. I kept running and running and running. Eventually I ran out of energy. I called a cab to take me home. She was waiting at the door when I got there. She asked to come in – my brain said no. I said yes. Yes.

She told me that she came to talk to me, that seeing me reminded her that she had left many things unsaid. I filled with joy, thinking that this was the moment that all my pain ended, this was the moment that she would come home. She had different plans for the conversation. She told me that the calls I made were making her uncomfortable. She told me that I could never talk to her or see her again. She knew that I missed her. I missed her so much. She told me she only came to say goodbye. Goodbye.

I didn't want goodbye, I wanted forever. I wanted her to be home, with me. I wanted her to make the bed five times with me, to turn off the lights those 17, annoying times. I wanted her to give me perfect kisses. I wanted her acceptance; I needed her acceptance. When she walked out the door, all the progress I had made in the past few months went with her. I haven't stopped thinking about her since then, and I doubt she'll ever leave my mind. She'll stay now.

She changed my life forever; I haven't decided yet if that is a good thing or a bad thing. My brain constantly screams at me to clean, to arrange, to have order. My brain wants me to make the bed, but I don't make the bed anymore. I sleep with the lights on.

GIRLS, TOGETHER

we were never girls together
    we did not climb jungle gyms or braid each other's hair
    I did not spend the night in your childhood bedroom,
giggling until the sun rose
    we did not discuss our first crushes
    or our first loves or first heart breaks
    you and I were never girls together

instead, we met as old crones
    days of jungle gyms and firsts were long behind us
    yet there are days that I forget
    that we did not always find peace in each other
    that you were not always there to cry, laugh, celebrate
with
    that you met me after the world had hardened my heart
    that we, together, became girls again

we may have never been girls together

at least not in the sense of true, young girlhood
but with you in my life
I feel the little girl in me smile

THE VIEW FROM HIS
SHOULDERS

I don't remember the last time I sat on my father's shoulders. It's not as if we declared "This is the last time you'll be picked up and allowed to watch the world from up high. Tomorrow you will be stuck on your own two feet for good." Instead, my father placed me back on the earth one final time, neither of us knowing we were marking the end of an era.

While I don't remember the last time I sat on my father's shoulders, I remember many of the times before. There's the annual 4th of July firework shows, or one of the many walks through the water park, or all the times he carried me to the car after a family get together or play date.

As a young girl, I remember feeling on top of the world. In a way, I guess I was on top of the world – for most of my childhood, my dad *was* my world. He'd pick me up, place me on those strong shoulders, and I would gaze farther out than I ever could on my two short legs. For a moment, I got to see exactly what he saw. He'd carry me anywhere – around parks or malls, through library aisles or pumpkin patches. And in all those rides he gave, he never once complained.

Once the literal shoulder rides ended, the metaphorical ones began. Where my father used to pick me up and let me be carried around, now he bore the heavier weight of an adolescent child. He listened and advised with patience while I ranted endlessly about bullying or my special interest of the moment. He took on the weight of my life and the chaos that I tended to bring along with me. While I spent hours explaining to him why I absolutely had to have a certain book or album or concert ticket, he gave me his full attention. When I needed someone to drive me to a birthday party or a mall hang out, he volunteered.

As I grew into an adult and left home behind, he still bore the brunt of my stories. He guided me through college applications, multiple moves, medical crises, and my first job applications. When I felt like giving up, he'd remind me that I was smart and strong and capable. When I needed help, he dove in to rescue me. He stood by my side for all of life's biggest moments, always believing I could do it myself while also being ready to support me as needed.

Life continued. The two of us always able to fall back into easy conversation. We danced at my wedding, shared drinks over my first home, travelled together, and made lasting memories. Everywhere we went, I walked alongside him. Long gone were the days of him carrying me around, but I cherished the relationship we built as two adults. We reminisced on what used to be and the days of shoulder rides and skinned knees but remained excited for all the moments we hadn't yet shared.

It's been years since I last sat up high and let my dad carry me around. It's been years since I got to see the view from 6 feet up. Yet no matter how much time has passed, I'll always remember fondly the view from his shoulders.

MUSINGS ON THE WORLD

I will warn you before you enter this section – these works are the closest I'll ever get to standing on a soapbox. If you know me in real life, you know that I am extremely passionate about my thoughts and opinions. That is not to say that I don't invite opposition – I will happily debate (politely!) with others, even if we appear to be polar opposites in every way.

As an American who has lived through the 2000 election, the 9/11 terrorist attacks and subsequent war on terror, multiple presidents (each more annoying than the last), economic upheaval and recession, the rampant rise of school shootings, the BLM and other protest-based civil rights movements, endless debate around the rights of immigrants, and more, I have been forced in many ways to reflect on the state of the world as I know it. There are a lot of things about our world, both in and out of the United States, that is deeply fucked up. I could rant for literal hours about how frustrated I am at the state of affairs, at how quickly people are to anger these days.

In many ways, these stories were a way to channel both my rage and my (annoying) optimism about the world and specifically America. There is so much I want to say here, so much that I want to get off my chest, but I know better than to rant endlessly about topics that folks probably don't want to hear about.

In setting up this section though, there remains one point that I want to offer up to you, the reader.

I thought about turning this into a story of its own, but instead I decided to let it live as the introduction, to let it frame myself and my opinions and life compass. So here goes...

We have forgotten how to engage in healthy debate and conversation with one another. We have entirely abandoned polite disagreement and instead moved closer to complete hostility. People no longer listen to, comprehend, understand, or truly *hear* one another. People only care about being the loudest voice, fuck being right or nice, just be the loudest opinion in the room.

I was raised by a man who taught me, every day, to listen to the world around me and to respect the opinions of others. He told me that it was okay – and HEALTHY – to surround myself with people with different backgrounds and opinions. I strived my entire life to be a tolerant person, to be someone who could engage in thoughtful debate with others. Unfortunately, many others missed that memo.

Nuance died years ago. The general populace decided that opinions and beliefs only exist in black and white. And you know what? That's bullshit. Humanity exists in the gray area. Progress exists in the gray area. Tolerance and acceptance live in the gray area.

I digress. Thank you for coming to my TED Talk. I hope you enjoy the stories in this section and enjoy the collection as a whole. I thank you all for entertaining the ramblings of a mad woman.

THE HUMAN SPIRIT

there is a phrase about humanity
  the indomitable human spirit.
  this idea that
  no matter the place
  no matter the time
  no matter the circumstances
  our base humanity encourages us -
  to persevere,
  to conquer,
  to overcome.

throughout history
  we use this phrase to describe moments of conquest
  moments of survival
  moments of success
  we use it to discuss the great triumphs of man
  the sacrifices of a martyr
  the accomplishments of an athlete

. . .

but the true beauty of this quality
      is not found on a field of battle or sport
      it is in the tender moments
      the couple found embracing in the grave
      the children who help an old woman cross the road

52

and in those moments
      I know hope is not lost

THROUGH THE FOREIGNER'S EYES

Born and raised in the foothills of Appalachia, I was no stranger to beauty. I spent my childhood playing in the yard, my adolescence exploring the mountains, and my adulthood traveling across the United States seeing new landscapes and cities. My travels took me to many corners of this country - from the fast-paced streets of NYC to the natural wonders of southern Utah to the towering Douglas firs in the Pacific Northwest. From a natural beauty standpoint, America shined bright.

Despite that, I found myself hating the country I lived in. Well, perhaps hate was too strong of a word for this feeling. I felt America sat full of endless potential, but rampant individualism kept that potential locked away. Political, religious, and social upheaval, and constantly feeling at arms against my fellow Americans built this feeling of ire towards the only country I had ever called home. And these feelings continued to grow, especially as I found myself in other countries and saw their society through my rose-colored, tourist glasses.

Then I spent the afternoon with a group of tourists, folks that travelled to America from countries that I had and hadn't yet visited. Over drinks, they described their America and, lord, how my America paled in comparison to theirs.

They noticed the small moments that I took for granted. One person stated, "Americans are so friendly. You all are so open to helping people, especially here in the southern US."

I gaped at them. In my mind, Americans were quick to anger, brisk, abrupt. Sure, we would give anyone directions when asked on the street. And, alright, we would happily give you a laundry list of activities to do in our towns. And, of course, we loved meeting folks from different places and chatting with them. In noticing these small interactions, I started to rewire my view of Americans but still, overall, believed other places to be better than this.

Our conversation moved on to other topics, but at some point, I asked, "So, where have you travelled so far in the States? Are you going anywhere else before heading home?"

One of them spoke about the same national parks I visited years prior in Utah and Washington. Their eyes lit up with utter amazement. The national parks paved an even ground between us - I wholeheartedly agreed that our natural beauty was incredible and would even go so far as to say it was the best part of America.

Then they surprised me. They spoke of the unbroken sky and watching the sunset over the Midwest, watching miles of corn stalks waving in the breeze. They talked about the suburban sprawl style of living and how it differed from their centralized city models. All in all, their list of amazing or impressive or cool parts of America were the same parts that I (and many of my fellow Americans) viewed as mundane and unimportant.

Several drinks - and a full day of suggestions from me - later, I parted ways with my new friends. I found myself taking a moment to appreciate the parts of this country that I took for granted.

Don't misunderstand, America remains a greatly flawed

and complex country. We are divisive, individualistic, and quick to push our neighbor down if it will benefit us. Our politics run amok, the economy stands on stilts, and cohorts of people across the country would like to see us return to an era of shame rather than strive forward into a beautiful future.

But as I walk into each new day, I remind myself that hope is not entirely lost in these United States. I remind myself of the view through the foreigner's eyes.

STREAM OF CONSCIOUSNESS

Why am I here?

What did I come into this room for?

Where the fuck did I put my phone?

Why did I cut off that friendship? Were they really *that* bad? Was I *that* blind?

Why do people do bad things? Are some people predisposed to be evil or do they consciously decide?

What should I eat for dinner tonight?

Why do we have to decide what to eat every single day? Why has no one come up with systems or plans to make this easier?

Why do children get cancer? Actually, why does *anyone* get cancer?

Why do politicians lie all the time? Do they think we're all stupid and don't see right through them?

Why do people believe anything they read on the internet? No, seriously. Why are we believing that babies are cuddling tigers in a forest in India? It's AI for Christ's sake!

Why did I take that job? Do I even like what I do? Should I go back to grad school? No, I don't like school... And I have no money...

Why am I sad all the time? Should I take another online quiz for depression? Also, I think I have ADHD.

Why does my cat eat cardboard? Can cats die from eating cardboard? How would I even stop him from eating cardboard?

Why does my dog bark at the grass? Is it bugs or are they just stupid?

Why won't my mom listen to me?

Why did he leave me?

Why does the sun rise every day? How does the universe work?

Why did NASA stop sending humans to space? Good thing I gave up on becoming an astronaut.

Why do so many people accept the existence of billionaires?

Why are my property taxes so high? Why are my income taxes so high? Why does the government constantly misuse my tax dollars? I'm sick of sending bombs to the Middle East when my local schools don't have textbooks.

Why are there so many kinds of apples? And why are some green while others are different shades of red? What makes apples red?

Why are there so many kinds of soda? Or chips? Or any junk food? Who asked for this much variety? It's overwhelming.

Who the fuck is buying coconut scented bleach?

Why do people hurt others?

Why are weddings so damn expensive these days?

Why do people think fighting is healthy? When did discussing things like adults go out of style?

Why don't they love me? If I work hard enough, do you think they'll love me?

Why do I always believe in myself, even with the odds stacked against me?

How do others go on every day with smiles on their faces?

Why do we still support one another? What makes certain communities so tight knit? How do I build that in my own community?

Why do I still feel optimistic, despite all the *gestures around* everything?

Why can't I stop myself from feeling hope? Even when the world seems determined to burn, I'm still here finding silver linings.

I'm glad I'm still here. I'm glad you're still here. I'm glad we all found ways to feel hope.

THE END.

ACKNOWLEDGMENTS

I hate this part of the book writing process LOL. I'm always convinced I'm going to forget someone important, so if you read this and go "what the fuck, Grace?!" I'M SORRY I DID MY BEST.

Firstly, to my incredible husband who insists that I am a great writer, even on days where I am very loudly bitching about being a bad writer. I love you forever and ever, Jesse.

To my incredible family – my sister Katie (who had to deal with ALL of my creative or marketing questions), my brother-in-law Kurt, my mother-in law, my dad, my father-in-law, Paul, and the entire extended Finnick, Miller, and Manders clans. You all make it possible for me to keep writing by being the best support system a girl could wish for.

To my amazing friends – Anna, Josh, Leah, Jordan, Ryan, Zoe, Claude, etc. Thank you for always making me laugh and listening to me talk endlessly about my latest writing. Thank you for all the hilarious parties and get togethers. I am endlessly blessed to have each of you in my life.

To my kitties, Minny and Molly. I really wish you both would shut the fuck up and let me focus sometimes, but I am grateful for the purrs and snuggles I got along the way.

To my ApollyCon 2025 Solo Support Crew. You all have made me feel so incredibly welcomed and loved in the book community. I am forever grateful that I saw the Facebook comment that led me to you all. Thank you all for encouraging me through everything this year and for your constant loud support of my writing and my bookish Instagram account.

To Kate Dramis and the Auburn crew, damn I'm so glad I connected with you all this year. Kate, thanks for being incredibly cool and not getting annoyed when I ask you stupid questions or otherwise bombard your Instagram DMs with my emotions. To all the Auburn crew – Ash, Victoria, Tris, Miranda, et al. – thanks for taking me under your wings at multiple events. I am very thankful and grateful to know you all.

And finally, to you, the reader. Thank you for picking up my book. Thank you for reading my words. Thank you for letting me cling just a little longer to this insane dream of being an author.

MY WRITING PLAYLIST

Dum Spiro, Spero playlist

Maine – Noah Kahan
Let Down – Mack Lorén
Exit Music (For A Film) - Radiohead
Godlight – Noah Kahan
My Tears Are Becoming a Sea – M83
Time – Hans Zimmer
Day One (Interstellar Theme) - Hans Zimmer
Purpose is Glorious – Natalie Holt
Experience – Ludovico Einaudi
Pathos – Ludovico Einaudi
On the Nature of Daylight – Max Richter, Lorenz Dangel
Sweet Heat Lightning – Gregory Alan Isakov
Ribs – Lorde
Vienna – Billy Joel
It's Called: Freefall – Paris Paloma
No Surprises (feat. Gregory Alan Isakov) - Jeremiah Fraites
In This Shirt – The Irrepressibles

ABOUT THE AUTHOR

Grace is a software engineer by day and aspiring author by night. She reads voraciously and enjoys writing everything from literary fiction to romance to fantasy. She is a hopeless romantic who blames it on falling for her high school sweetheart.

Grace lives in north Georgia with her husband and their two cats. You can find more information at her website: authorgracemanders.com.